D0515444

Groundwood Books / House of Anansi Press
groundwoodbooks.com

We acknowledge for their financial support of our publishing
program the Canada Council for the Arts, the Ontario Arts
Council and the Government of Canada.

Canada Council **Conseil des Arts**
for the Arts **du Canada**

ONTARIO ARTS COUNCIL
CONSEIL DES ARTS DE L'ONTARIO
an Ontario government agency
un organisme du gouvernement de l'Ontario

With the participation of the Government of Canada | **Canadä**
Avec la participation du gouvernement du Canada

Library and Archives Canada Cataloguing in Publication
Sher, Emil, author
Away / Emil Sher ; illustrated by Qin Leng.
Issued in print and electronic formats.
ISBN 978-1-55498-483-1 (hardback). –
ISBN 978-1-55498-484-8 (pdf)
I. Leng, Qin, illustrator II. Title.
PS8587.H38535A95 201   jC813'.54   C2016-905854-9
C2016-905855-7

The illustrations were done in ink and watercolor.
Design by Michael Solomon
Printed and bound in Malaysia

MIX
Paper from
responsible sources
FSC® C012700
FSC
www.fsc.org

For Sophie and Molly,
and the gift of fatherhood – ES

For Mom and Dad – QL

Away

written by Emil Sher

illustrated by Qin Leng

Groundwood Books
House of Anansi Press
Toronto Berkeley

Good morning, Skip!
Your lunch is in
fridge.
Let's have one more
movie night
before you go.

WED	THU	FRI	SAT	SUN
3	4	5	6 Dr. Keipas @ 4:45	7 Hearing aid battery Busker festival
10	11	12	13	14
17	18	19	20	21
24	2			28
31				

Lonely Lester and I will have movie night

while you're gone.

I got B+ in math.
I'm not packing.
NOT EVER!

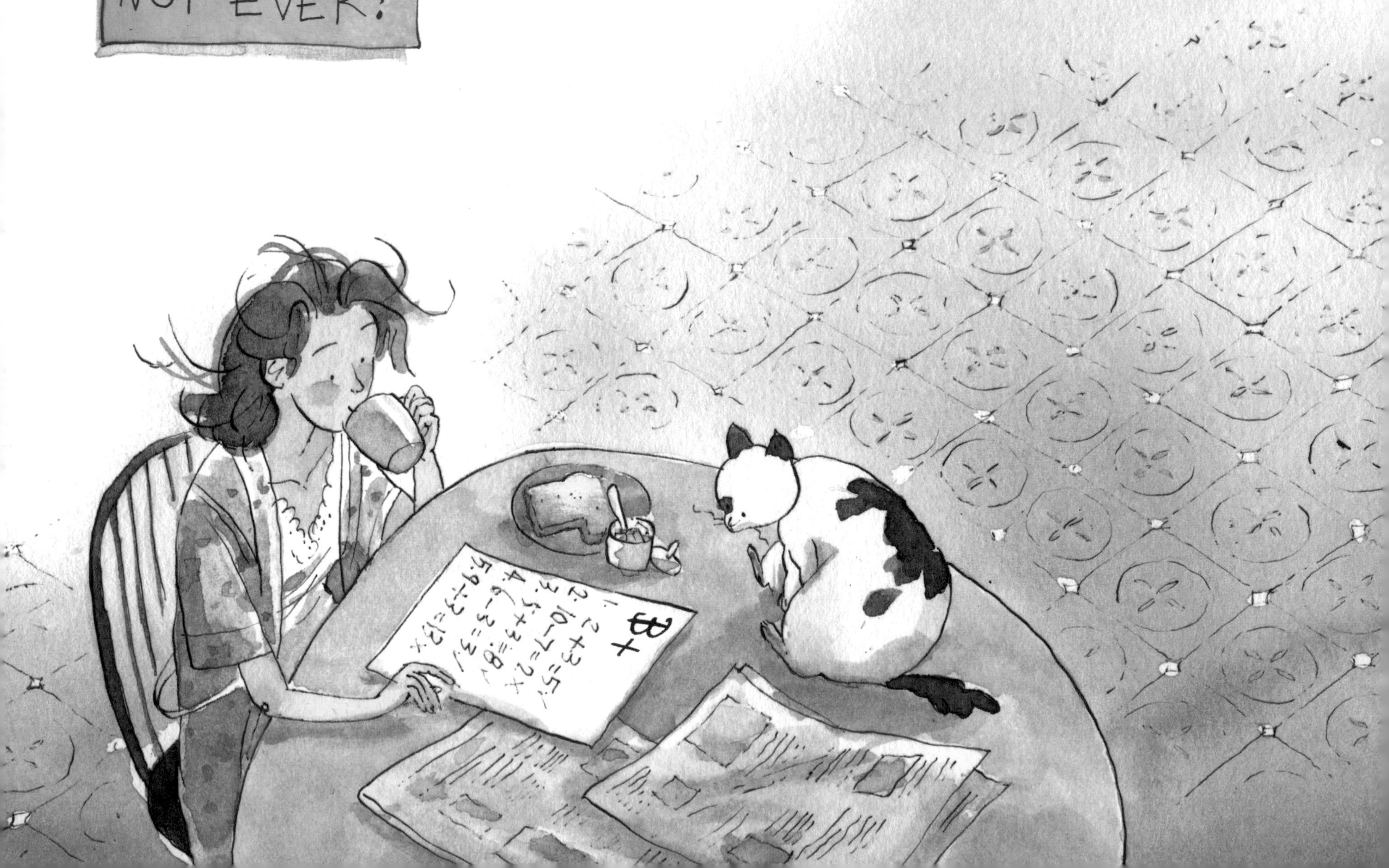

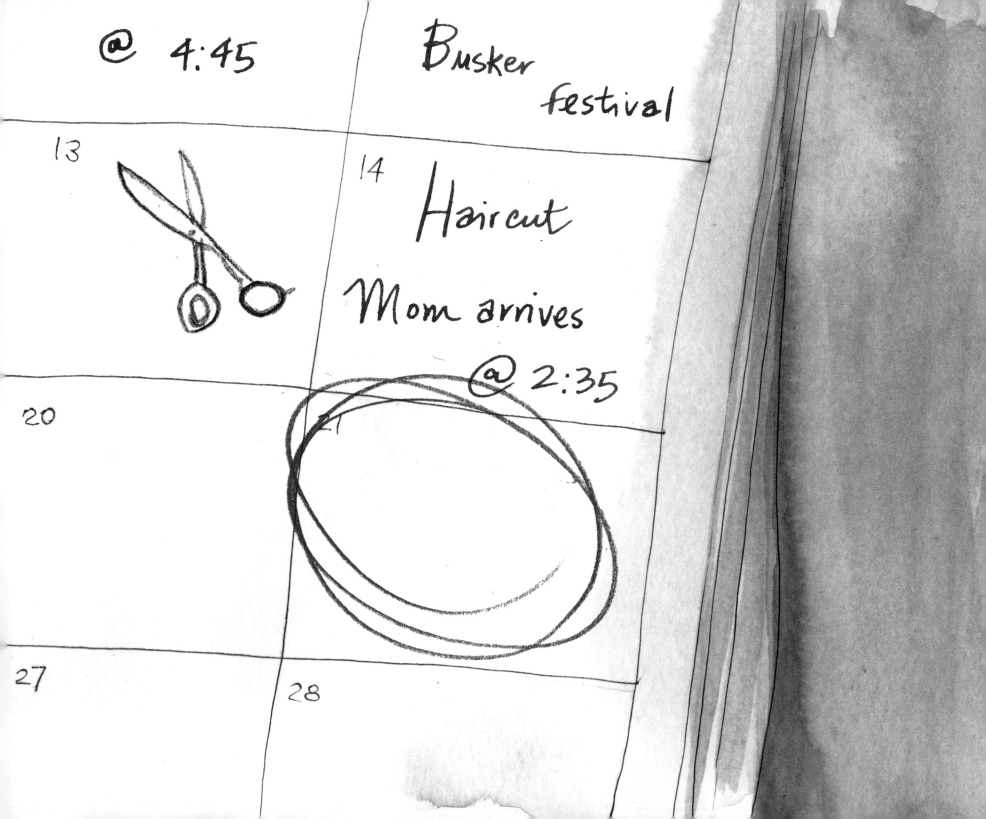

@ 4:45

Busker festival

13

14
Haircut

Mom arrives
@ 2:35

20

27

28

Mimsy showed me a picture of you. A 9 years old you.

A crying you. Holding a suitcase. And a fuzzy walrus.

I remember that walrus! My tears didn't last. My memories are as warm as biscuits.

Can I take the picture of you and the walrus?